a Charlie Brown Christmas

a Charlie Brown Christmas

by
Charles M. Schulz

adapted from a Bill Melendez production

WORLD PUBLISHING
TIMES MIRROR
NEW YORK

Published by The World Publishing Company
110 East 59th Street, New York City, New York 10022
Printed simultaneously in Canada
by Nelson, Foster & Scott Ltd.
Copyright © 1965 by United Feature Syndicate, Inc.

1972 Printing

Library of Congress Catalog Card Number: 66-13149
ISBN: 0-529-04874-4

Printed in the United States of America

WORLD PUBLISHING
TIMES MIRROR

To all who know
the true meaning of Christmas—
the children of
the world

"I think there must be something wrong with me, Linus. Christmas is coming, but I'm not happy. I don't feel the way I'm supposed to feel. I just don't understand Christmas. I guess I like getting presents, sending Christmas cards, and decorating trees, and all that, but I'm still not happy."

"Charlie Brown, you are the only person I know who can take a wonderful season like Christmas and turn it into a problem," said Linus.

"Look, Charlie Brown, those kids are forgetting their problems, so why don't you forget *yours?*"

"Charlie Brown!
Look
at
Snoopy!"

"If he can crack the whip
like that, maybe you should
consult him. Maybe he can straighten you out."
"I think I'll just go to bed," said Charlie Brown.

When Charlie Brown woke up the next day, his problem was still with him.

"I should see a doctor," he said. "I'll go to Lucy's psychiatric booth."

"Lucy, I'm in bad shape. Actually, my problem is Christmas. I just don't understand it; instead of feeling happy, I feel sort of let down."

"Charlie Brown, you need involvement. You need to get involved in
some real Christmas project. How
would you like to be the director of
our Christmas play?"

"Me?" said Charlie Brown. "You
mean me to be the director of the
Christmas play?"

"Sure, Charlie Brown. WE need a
director—YOU need involvement.
Don't worry, I'll be there to meet
you at the auditorium."

Charlie Brown had been reading the paper earlier.
"Home lighting and display contest. Spectacular! Super colossal!
Find the true meaning of Christmas!"
And then he found Snoopy decorating the doghouse.
"Even
my dog
has gone
commercial,"
he was thinking.

Then Charlie Brown's sister Sally asked him to write a letter to Santa Claus for her.

She dictated: "How is your wife? I've been very good this year so I shall enclose an extra-long list of things I want. Or perhaps you could just send me money, preferably tens and twenties."

Charlie Brown said, "Augh!"
"All I want is what I've got coming to me.
All I want is my fair share," said Sally.

Still later, Lucy was speaking at the auditorium.
"All right. Quiet everybody!
Our director will be here in a minute and we'll start rehearsal."
And in came Charlie Brown.

"Well it's real good seeing you all here. As you know we're going to put on this Christmas play. One of the first things to insure a good performance is STRICT attention to the director. And the actors must show spirit."

"That's not the kind of spirit I mean," said Charlie Brown, as the kids broke into a discotheque dance.

And in one corner of the stage, Lucy was saying, "Snoopy, you'll have to be all the animals in our play. Can you be a sheep?"

Snoopy replied, "Baa," and saluted.

"Augh," she said, "I've been kissed by a dog! I have dog germs! Get hot water! Get some disinfectant! Get some iodine!"

Then he slupped her.

Charlie Brown waved his megaphone. "All right! Script girl, hand out the parts!"

Lucy gave Linus his lines and a costume. "Linus, you've got to get rid of that stupid blanket. And here, memorize these lines."

"I can't memorize these lines. This is ridiculous," said Linus.

"Linus, memorize them and be ready to recite when your time comes."

"Lucy, give me one good reason why I should memorize this."

"Linus, I'll give you *five* good reasons: one, two, three, four, five!" she said, pointing to her fist.

"Christmas is not only getting too commercial, it's also getting too dangerous," said Linus.

Charlie Brown raised his megaphone: "All right, places everybody. Let's have it quiet."

The spirit
of the actors
was growing by leaps
and bounds, with
Snoopy showing
the way.

"Now look . . . if we're ever to get
this play off the ground, we've got
to have some cooperation!"
Charlie Brown was disgusted
and slammed down
his megaphone.

"Lucy, it's ALL wrong."

"Look, Charlie Brown, let's face it. We all know that Christmas is a big commercial racket. It's run by a big Eastern syndicate, you know."

"Well, Lucy, this is one play that's not gonna be commercial."

Charlie Brown said, "We need a Christmas tree."

"Hey! Perhaps a tree *is* what we need," said Lucy. "A great big, shiny aluminum Christmas tree. That's it, Charlie Brown. You get the tree."

"Okay, Lucy, I'll take Linus with me. The rest of you practice your lines."

"Get the biggest aluminum tree you can find," said Lucy. "Maybe painted pink . . . Yeah! Do something right for a change, Charlie Brown."

"Charlie Brown, this really brings
Christmas close to a person."

Charlie Brown looked till he found a real live tree.

"Linus, this little green one here seems to need a home."

"I don't know, Charlie Brown. Remember what Lucy said. . . . This doesn't seem to fit the modern spirit."

"I don't care, Linus. We'll decorate it and it'll be just right for our play. Besides, I think it needs me."

When Charlie Brown and Linus
got back to the auditorium,
Lucy looked at them in disgust.
"Charlie Brown,
you were supposed to get a good tree.
Can't you even tell a GOOD tree from a poor tree?
You've been dumb before,
Charlie Brown,
but this time
you really did it."

Charlie Brown looked at
the sad little tree on the piano.
"Isn't there anyone who knows
what Christmas is all about?"
"Sure, Charlie Brown,"
said Linus, "I can tell you
what Christmas
is all about."

Then Linus, alone now on the stage, said, "Lights, please." When the spotlight was turned on, he spoke. "And there were in the same country shepherds . . .

. . . abiding in the field, keeping watch over their flock by night. And lo, the angel of the Lord came upon them, and the glory of the Lord shone round about them: and they were sore afraid. And the angel said unto them, Fear not: for, behold, I bring you good tidings of . . .

. . . great joy, which shall be to all people.
For unto you is born this day
in the city of David a Saviour,
which is Christ the Lord.
And this shall be a sign unto you;
Ye shall find the babe
wrapped in swaddling clothes, lying in . . .

. . . a manger. And suddenly there was with the angel
a multitude of the heavenly host
praising God, and saying,
Glory to God in the highest,
and on earth peace,
good will toward men."

"And that's what Christmas is all about, Charlie Brown," said Linus.

"Listen again," said Linus. "Go outside. Look up at the stars and listen."

Charlie Brown took up
his little tree and walked out.

"For, behold, I bring you
good tidings of great joy,
which shall be to all people.
For unto you is born this day
in the city of David a Saviour,
which is Christ the Lord.
And this shall be a sign unto you."

As he walked home, Charlie Brown
thought, "Linus is right! I won't let all this
commercialism spoil my Christmas."

"I'll take this little tree home and decorate it. I'll show them that it really will
work in our play."

When Charlie Brown got home with his little tree, Snoopy's doghouse was all decorated. Charlie Brown thought, "Augh, first prize, indeed! This commercial dog is not going to ruin my Christmas, either."

Charlie Brown picked out a decoration and
hung it on his tree. The tree drooped way over.
"I've killed it," said Charlie Brown.
He felt so sad that he went for a walk.

While he was gone, all the others came around.
Linus said, "It's not a bad little tree, really.
It just needs love."
He put his blanket around the tree.

The tree sprang back to life, and then
everyone began to hang ornaments on it.
The more they worked, the fuller and more
beautiful the tree became.

Then Charlie Brown came back.

"I told you that you needed involvement, Charlie Brown," said Lucy.
"Who needs a play, anyway? We need more people like Linus.
LOOK HOW HE MADE YOUR TREE GROW!"

"Charlie Brown is a blockhead, but he did get a nice tree, actually," said Lucy.

"A MERRY CHRISTMAS TO ALL," said Charlie Brown